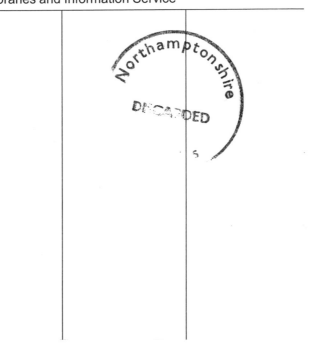

TREVOR'S BOAT HUNT
A RED FOX BOOK 0 09 945117 4

First published in Great Britain in 2003 by Red Fox,
an imprint of Random House Children's Books

1 3 5 7 9 10 8 6 4 2

Copyright © Rob Lewis, 2003

Set in Cheltenham Book Infant

Red Fox Books are published by Random House Children's Books,
61–63 Uxbridge Road, London W5 5SA,
a division of The Random House Group Ltd,
in Australia by Random House Australia (Pty) Ltd,
20 Alfred Street, Milsons Point, Sydney, NSW 2061, Australia,
in New Zealand by Random House New Zealand Ltd,
18 Poland Road, Glenfield, Auckland 10, New Zealand,
and in South Africa by Random House (Pty) Ltd,
Endulini, 5A Jubilee Road, Parktown 2193, South Africa

THE RANDOM HOUSE GROUP Limited Reg. No. 954009

www.**kids**at**randomhouse**.co.uk

Printed and bound in Singapore by Tien Wah Press

Trevor's Boat Hunt

by Rob Lewis

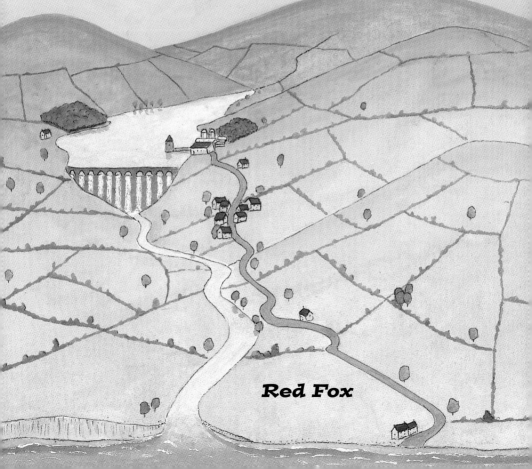

Red Fox

Trevor and his family were
having a picnic.

Trevor was sailing his boat in a pool.
Water was gushing out of a hole in the rocks
and was pushing his boat along. "Where does
all that water come from?" Trevor asked.

"It rains on the hill above," said Mum.
"Then it goes into the ground and comes out
through cracks in the rock like that one."

Trevor peered into the crack. With all that water coming out there must be lots of rain in the sky, Trevor thought.

Careful, Trevor, don't get your head stuck!

Then it started to rain.

"Talking about rain has made it rain!" said Trevor.

"Quick," said Dad. "Help us to pick up the picnic things, Trevor."

Silly rain!

Trevor carried the plates, his sister carried the cups. Then they all went home.

"Oh, no!" said Trevor when they got home.
"I've left my boat behind."

"It's too late to look for it now," said Dad.
"We'll go back for it tomorrow."

My boat!

Trevor watched the rain. It rained harder and harder.

"I hope my boat doesn't fill with water," he said.

The next day, Trevor and his family went
back to the pool.

Trevor looked for his boat, but it wasn't
there. "My boat has sunk," Trevor said,
sadly.

"I don't think so," said Dad. "A plastic boat will float even if it's full of water."

"Let's follow the stream," said Mum. "Maybe it has floated away after all that rain."

Maybe a fish has eaten it!

Trevor looked amongst the rocks in the stream, but he couldn't find his boat anywhere. Instead he found a long stick. "That might be useful," he said.

The stream got wider and wider until it became a river. Trevor looked all along the river bank but there was still no sign of his boat. Instead he found two plastic bottles. "These might be useful," he said.

A handy bottle!

The river flowed into a big lake. Dad said it was called a reservoir.

"I'll never find my boat now," Trevor groaned.

"Cheer up," said Mum. "The wind might have blown it across to the other side."

At the other side of the reservoir was a big dam. Water was pouring over the top, making a huge waterfall.

Can you see my boat?

"I hope Trevor's boat hasn't gone down there," said Trevor's sister. "It would get smashed to pieces."

Trevor didn't want to think about his boat being smashed to pieces.

Instead he looked at a tower in the water.

"That's where water is taken out for people to use," explained Dad. "It goes down that big pipe."

The family went for a closer look.

There was a lot of rubbish
floating on the water, but some
metal bars were stopping it
from going down the pipe.

Trevor peered down at the rubbish.
He was hoping he might see his boat. There
were bits of leaves, glass bottles and plastic
cartons but there was no sign of his boat.

Instead, Trevor used his stick to pull out a plastic bag with pretty patterns on it. "That might be useful," he said.

25

Next to the water tower were some square ponds. "That's where all the water is filtered," said Mum. "All the tiny bits of mud settle at the bottom of those ponds so the water is clear when it comes out of our taps."

Trevor hoped his boat hadn't been filtered.

"They put chemicals, such as chlorine, in the water to kill any nasty bugs," said Dad. "Then it's piped to our houses, ready for us to drink."

There was still no sign of Trevor's boat.

That night Trevor spent a long time in the bathroom. He was wondering if bits of his boat might come out of the tap.

Then he looked down the
toilet just in case there were
bits of his boat floating in the water.

The next day, Trevor and his family went to the beach. It was not a sandy beach. All Trevor could see was mud.

"This is where the river joins the sea," said Mum.

Trevor watched the river in case he saw his boat.

Suddenly he saw a blue boat funnel in the water.

"It's my boat!" he cried.

My boat!

Dad used a net to fish it out of the water.
But it was only a piece of plastic pipe.

"I wonder if my boat has gone out to sea,"
Trevor said, sadly. "I'll never find it now."

"Cheer up, Trevor," said Dad. "Maybe it
has been washed up on the beach."

"Maybe it has been eaten by a shark,"
said Trevor's sister.

Trevor wished his sister had been eaten
by a shark.

As Trevor walked along the beach there was less mud and more sand. There was a lot of seaweed and bits of wood.

There were also bottle tops and dead crabs. But there was no sign of his boat.

Instead, Trevor found a piece of net and a piece of wood with a hole in it.

"These might be useful," he said.

Trevor watched the clouds
blow in from the sea. Somewhere
out there was his boat.

"Never mind, Trevor," said Mum.
"I'm sure we can get you a new boat."
But Trevor was smiling. He had just
had an idea.

When he got home he rushed up to his
room. He stayed there a long time.

"What's Trevor doing?" Dad wondered.

"Maybe he's feeling seasick," said
his sister.

KEEP OUT!

Trevor's Room

Then Trevor appeared.

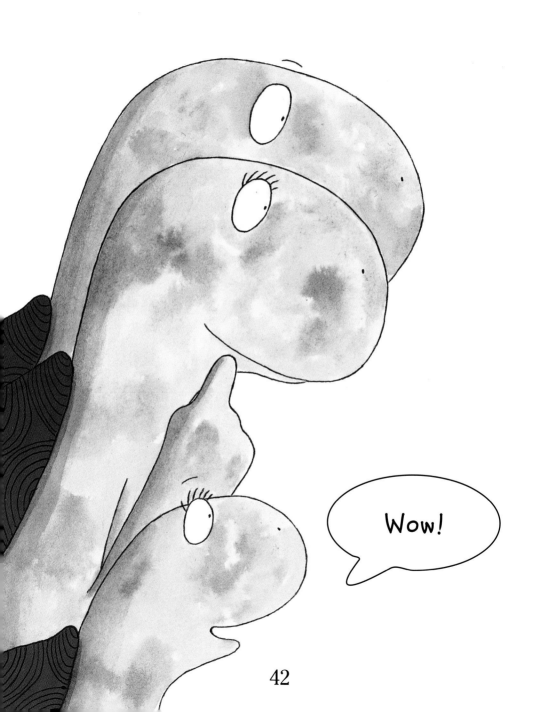

42

"I don't need my old boat any more,"
he said. "Look! I've made a new one!"

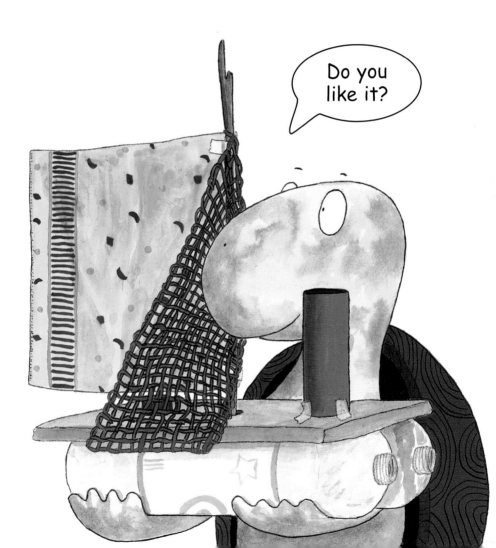

Trevor saw that water travels a long way from when it falls as rain to when it reaches the sea. He also discovered how the water we use is filtered before it comes out of the tap. You try it!

YOU WILL NEED: two empty jam jars, earth, kitchen paper, a funnel

1. Fill a jam jar with clean water and add a handful of earth. Shake it up. Look at the colour of the water.

2. Next, line a funnel with kitchen paper.

3. Place the funnel over a clean, empty jam jar. Pour the muddy water into the funnel. The kitchen paper filters out the dirt.

earth

jam jar

kitchen paper

funnel (cone with an open tube at bottom)

All living things need water to live. People use water to drink, to cook, and to keep clean and healthy. How else do we use water?

4. Leave the water to settle overnight. What does it look like now?

Fill a glass with water and take a good look at it. Can you guess how old it is? It could have fallen from the sky as rain last week.

All of our water comes from the rain and melted snow.

The water cools and makes new clouds.

Water never stops moving in the water cycle.

e water falls
wn from the
uds as rain
snow.

The sun heats the water so that it **evaporates**, or changes into a gas. It goes up into the air, like the steam from a kettle.

It fills rivers and streams and flows into the lakes, seas and oceans.

Rob Lewis

How did you get the idea for this story? I live close to four reservoirs and a small water plant where you can see the filter beds like in this story. Also, my sons like to sail paper boats in the rocky streams near where I live. Very often the boats get lost or sink.

What do you like to draw most? I like to draw landscapes and Trevor. He's my favourite character to draw.

Where is your favourite place to draw? In the garden when it's not raining. I painted this book in winter so I had to work indoors in my studio.

What do you do if you get stuck on a drawing? I go and eat some chocolate or cheese!

What is your favourite picnic food? I like cheese and crackers. Trevor's favourite is lettuce sandwiches (see *Tidy Up, Trevor!*).

46

Did you play with boats when you were a child? Did you like to make things like Trevor? I didn't play with boats, but I made model villages out of plastic bottles, cardboard, and papier-mâché.

What did you like most when you were a child? What did you hate? I liked building dens in the field behind our house. I hated piano lessons. Now, I play guitar instead.

Can I be an illustrator like you? Yes, but you must practise drawing whenever you can. Take a sketchbook with you wherever you go and draw, draw, draw!

Will you try and write or draw a story too?

Why not visit Rob's website for more fun experiments to do with water: www.rob-lewis.co.uk

Let your ideas take flight with
Flying Foxes

Moonchap by Mary Murphy

All the Little Ones – and a Half by Mary Murphy

Jed's Really Useful Poem by Ragnhild Scamell and Jane Gray

Jake and the Red Bird by Ragnhild Scamell and Valeria Petrone

Pam's Maps by Pippa Goodhart and Katherine Lodge

Slow Magic by Pippa Goodhart and John Kelly

Rama's Return by Lisa Bruce and Katja Bandlow

Magic Mr Edison by Andrew Melrose and Katja Bandlow

Rosa and Galileo by Anne Cottringer and Lizzie Finlay

A Tale of Two Wolves by Susan Kelly and Lizzie Finlay

That's Not Right! by Alan Durant and Katharine McEwen

Sherman Swaps Shells by Jane Clarke and Ant Parker

Only Tadpoles Have Tails by Jane Clarke and Jane Gray

Digging for Dinosaurs by Judy Waite and Garry Parsons

Shadowhog by Sandra Ann Horn and Mary McQuillan

The Magic Backpack by Julia Jarman and Adriano Gon

Don't Let the Bad Bugs Bite! by Lindsey Gardiner

Trevor's Boat Hunt by Rob Lewis